Shooting the Rapids

A novel by

Paul Kropp

HIP-JR.

HIP Junior
Copyright © 2006 by High Interest Publishing

Library and Archives Canada Cataloguing in Publication

Kropp, Paul, 1948–
    Shooting the rapids / Paul Kropp.

(HIP jr)
ISBN 1-897039-20-4

I. Title. II. Series.

PS8571.R772S49 2006   jC813'.54   C2006-903378-1

General editor: Paul Kropp
Text design and typesetting: Laura Brady
Illustrations drawn by: Catherine Doherty
Cover design: Robert Corrigan

2 3 4 5 6 7   10 11 12 13 14

Printed and bound in Canada

High Interest Publishing is an imprint of the
Chestnut Publishing Group

When dad gets hurt on a canoe trip, his two sons have to get him back to town. But when the boys get lost, the hours turn into days in the wilderness. Can they reach help in time?

CHAPTER 1

An Easy Start

My dad likes to goof around. Sometimes his jokes are good. Sometimes they're dumb. When we started our canoe trip, Dad came up with a really dumb joke.

"Hey, guys," he said. "How do you like my hat?"

He had the canoe over his head.

Real funny, eh? I didn't bother to laugh. My brother, Timmy, just shook his head. He was still mad. Dad had made him leave his Gameboy at home.

So my dad laughed at his own joke. That's how our canoe trip started — my dad goofing around. It was my dad goofing around that made all the trouble later on. But that was later.

My dad took us north on one canoe trip each summer. He told Mom it was good for us. He said he needed time to "hang out" with his boys.

I'm Connor and I'm almost twelve. I'd rather hang out with my friends than go on a canoe trip. But no one asked me. Instead, we drive for a day, then sleep in a cheap motel. At the crack of dawn, our canoe goes into the water. Then it's three days of paddling. Three days of trying to catch fish. Three days of bugs. And three days of Timmy whining.

I just wish Dad would let Timmy bring his Gameboy. At least he'd be quiet.

We got our canoe into the water. Then Dad piled in the stuff we'd need. The plan was to canoe for four days and go 80 km. We started just northwest of La Ronge. Then we'd follow Pinehouse Lake up to the Churchill River. We had a tent, sleeping bags and enough food to get by.

I looked out over the lake. The sun was just
coming up, and the air was still. I could hear some
birds singing. A little wind whistled through the
jack pines.

"Pretty nice," my dad said. He saw me looking
out over the water.

"Yeah," I agreed. I had to admit it was beautiful.
On a good morning, it was like a postcard.

"Glad you came?"

"I guess," I said. "But I still miss my friends."

Dad smiled. "Maybe next year we'll bring them. We'll get three canoes. Then you and Timmy can each bring two friends."

Maybe next year is my dad's big line. The trouble is, next year is always the same. Dad forgets, every year.

We started paddling down the lake. Dad always gets the back. I usually start in the front. Timmy sits in the middle, doing nothing. When I get tired, Timmy takes my spot. The plan was to canoe 15 km, halfway to the Churchill River. On a nice day like this, that should have been easy.

"You know, this route is famous," Dad said, just before lunch.

"Was it in a movie?" Timmy asked.

"No, better than that," Dad explained. "It was in history."

I groaned. Timmy shook his head. Our dad is a history teacher. He's even a history teacher when we go camping.

"Lots of explorers took this route," my dad began.

6

Timmy cut him off. "Who?"

"Old-time explorers," I told him. "Way back in history."

"Like in the 1950s?"

Dad and I both laughed. Timmy is only eight — and he's a dumb eight, if you ask me.

"Anyhow, those guys would paddle their canoes, just like us," Dad went on. "They'd go up north to trade for furs. They'd set up trading posts. . . ."

Dad went on like this for maybe half an hour. He knows a lot about history. It was just before lunch when Timmy stopped my dad's lesson.

"Hey, Dad," Timmy cut in. "Can we do some whitewater?"

"What?" my dad asked. He didn't like his history lessons being cut off.

"Whitewater . . . you know, like rapids. I saw this show on TV —"

This time my dad cut off Timmy. "Forget it," he snapped. "Not until you've had lessons. And not until you're sixteen or maybe twenty."

"Dad!" Timmy whined. The word came out all stretched — *daaad*! "It'd be fun."

Dad chose to ignore that. "Now where was I?" my dad said. Then the history lesson went on.

After three hours, we stopped for lunch and some rest. Mom had packed sandwiches for us and a pile of cookies. Then dad did a lesson on rocks and stuff like that, but I dozed off. I had a dream about a boat shooting over rocks, and that woke me up.

We paddled all afternoon. The wind was at our backs, so we made good time. Before dark, we had reached our 15 km goal. We had gone past the town and past the narrows. But we had not seen another person all day. There were float planes over our heads but not one other canoe on the lake.

Dad found a spot to camp for the night. It was on some dry land right beside some rapids. We could hear the water splashing against the rocks all night.

Timmy and I found wood for a fire. The one

great thing about a day of paddling — it makes you really hungry. We ate a half-dozen hamburgers, and then a ton of cookies.

"You guys want a bedtime story?" Dad asked. He's been telling us weird bedtime stories all our lives.

Timmy was too tired. I was too old.

"How about a bedtime joke?" Dad asked. "What do you say to a bear when it breaks into your camp?"

"I don't know. What?"

"Nothing. You just start running like crazy."

"That's not a joke," I said. "It's not funny."

"I'm saving the good stuff for tomorrow," Dad replied. "Wait till you see how funny I can be in the morning."

Dad wouldn't be funny in the morning, either. And when Dad *tried* to be funny, he almost got himself killed.

CHAPTER 2

"Dad, Dad, Are You Okay?"

Dad was always careful when we camped. He hung our food up in the trees. He kept a fire going through the night. He slept with a flashlight and a wooden stick "just in case of bears." As if a wood stick will fight off a bear.

As soon as we got up, my dad began to goof around.

"You guys want to hear a new bear joke?" he began.

We groaned. My brother is not a morning

11

person. And I hate jokes before breakfast.

"A bear breaks into camp," my dad began, "and chases two guys up a tree. The bear is growling and the guys are scared."

Timmy burped.

My dad went on. "So the first guy puts on his running shoes. Then the second guy says, 'Why the running shoes? You can't run faster than a bear.'"

Dad looked at us both. I guess we were getting to the punch line. "So the first guy says, 'I don't need to run faster than the bear. I just need to run faster than you!'"

I shook my head. Timmy burped again.

"Get it? I just have to run faster than you. If the bear gets the one guy . . ."

"Very funny, Dad," I told him. Bad jokes are a problem when your dad is a teacher.

Anyhow, Dad cooked us some pancakes for breakfast. He had to climb way up a cliff to where we built the fire. Then he came down with a big pile of pancakes. They were covered with jam and sugar, just the way we like them.

So we ate breakfast. About halfway into the pancakes, I *got* Dad's joke. I guess it was a little funny. Then we cleaned up our stuff and got ready to go. The weather wasn't so good. It was cloudy and the wind would be against us. Still, my dad had a plan. Four days of paddling, then two days at a camp. We always kept to the plan.

We got our stuff back in the canoe. Then my dad went over by the rapids. He took a pail for water to put out the fire. But when he got over there, Dad began goofing around.

"Hey, guys," he shouted to us. "Look over here!"

My dad was up on a big rock. He held a piece of wood in one hand. The wood was burning at one end, like a torch.

"I'm the Statue of Liberty!" Dad shouted.

Timmy really did laugh at that. I guess it was a kind of dumb eight-year-old joke.

Dad kept on. "Give me your poor, your tired, your —"

That's as far as he got. His foot slipped on a wet

rock. Dad lost his balance. For a second, I thought he was still joking. I thought he was pretending to slip on the rock.

But this was no joke. Dad was falling.

But that wasn't the worst part. Dad didn't just fall into the water. He fell head first and hit some rocks. Then he kind of rolled into the water.

"Dad!" Timmy cried.

"Stay here," I shouted. "I'm going in."

Fast as anything, I pulled off my sweater and

jumped into the water. I'm not a great swimmer but good enough. In twenty seconds, I reached my father.

Dad was out cold. A big cut on his head was bleeding like crazy. The water around him was turning red from the blood.

Now what? I said to myself. I knew I had to get Dad out of the water. That was number one. But I've never had a lifesaving course. So I tried to think — what do they do in the movies? Okay, wrap my arm around his neck and then drag him backwards.

It's easy in the movies. In real life, it's hard. My dad was floating, but he couldn't help me. I held him with my arm, but it was hard to kick beneath him and under the water. My other arm just kept splashing on the surface. My head kept sinking beneath the water. It felt like I was going nowhere.

It took a long time to get over to the shore. When I got close, Timmy threw me a rope. Then he pulled both Dad and me in.

I crawled up on the rocks, then coughed up the water in my lungs.

"Connor, help me!" my brother cried. He was trying to pull Dad up on shore all by himself.

I ran over beside him and grabbed Dad's other arm. "Pull!" I shouted.

With the two of us working together, we got Dad out of the water.

"Get the first aid kit," I shouted. Then I began coughing again.

Timmy ran to the canoe and began looking. It took him a long time. The first aid kit was packed in the bottom of a barrel. At last, Timmy came running back with it.

I searched through the kit. I needed a bandage, one of those big cloth bandages. Somehow we had to stop the bleeding. At last I found what I needed. I pressed the bandage to my dad's head. The bandage began to turn red from blood.

"Dad, Dad, are you okay?" Timmy asked.

I shot my little brother a look. Of course Dad was not okay. He was knocked right out, but at least he was still breathing.

"He's breathing," I told him.

"Dad, Dad . . . " Timmy repeated, and then he started to cry.

CHAPTER 3

Which Way?

There was no time for crying. Dad was hurt, bad, and we had to get help. We were just two kids, a long way from anywhere. We needed help, fast.

"Get the cell phone," I shouted to Timmy. I kept the bandage on Dad's head. The worst bleeding had almost stopped.

Timmy opened up two packs, then found the phone. He pushed the power button, then waited. "Nothing," he said.

"Let me try," I said. I pushed the power button again and still got nothing. Dad had forgotten to charge the phone.

"Okay, so we've got to paddle back," I said. "It took us a day to get here. It'll take us a day to get back."

"A day when Dad paddled. Not just us," Timmy said. I could tell he was about to cry again.

"Would you stop!" I shouted. "We're going to

get some help. We might even find somebody to help on the way."

"Yeah, I guess." Timmy sniffled.

"And the bleeding has stopped," I said. "That's a little good news. I'm going to tie a bandage around his head. You empty out the middle of the canoe. We're going to need room to get him in."

Timmy went over to the canoe and began pulling stuff out. If we got back in a day, we wouldn't need a tent. We wouldn't need all our food. We wouldn't need the little stove. We wouldn't need the barrel with books and games. The less stuff we had, the easier it would be to paddle.

"Ditch the tent," I told him. "And half the food. Then spread a sleeping bag out for Dad, right in the middle."

In no time, the canoe was ready. Timmy came over and took Dad's legs. I grabbed him under the arms. Then we dragged him to the canoe and tried to lift him in. No luck. Dad was too heavy.

"Okay, you get in the water and tip the canoe," I said. "I'll kind of roll Dad in."

This plan worked. We covered Dad with another sleeping bag to keep him warm. Isn't that the first rule of first aid? Keep the victim warm. Now what was the second rule?

"Okay, you get in front," I told my brother. "I'll paddle from the back." The stronger paddler gets the back. Usually, that's Dad. But now it was me.

We pushed out into the lake. In no time, we could feel the breeze and the current.

"Which way?" Timmy asked.

"The way we came," I said.

"Which way? Which way did we come?"

I looked at the trees and the shore. We had just come here yesterday, but now it all looked strange. We had come at sundown. Now it was morning, and the sky was grey. All I could see was the pile of stuff we left on the shore.

"Wait," I shouted.

I went into Dad's pack and found a map and a compass. That was good. But nothing on the map made sense. That was bad. There were all these lakes, all these lines on the paper. And what do you do with a compass?

"Which way?" Timmy shouted.

"Let me think," I said.

We were drifting with the wind and the current. Was that good? Was the current with us yesterday?

I put the compass on the map. Then I set it up so the N lined up with the big pointer. Up north there was only the Churchill River. But south of us was the town of Pinehouse. We knew there'd be help in the town. All we had to do was follow the edge of the lake. The town couldn't be more than 5 or 10 km away. We should be there in a couple of hours.

"Stay by the shore," I shouted. "Aim towards those rocks, then keep going."

So we started paddling. When Dad was with us, paddling was easy. He did most of the work. Timmy and I would just trade off up in front. The front isn't so bad, really. You just have to paddle so the canoe goes straight.

But the guy in back has to work. I paddled on my right side, then switched to my left. In an hour, I was aching. In two hours, I was ready to quit. Timmy was worse. I think he was crying for the last half hour.

"Okay, steer to the shore," I said. "We'll take a break."

When we got close, Timmy jumped out to pull us in. The water was deeper than he thought, and he got soaked. Still, it felt good to be on dry land.

"Cookies," Timmy wailed. "I need cookies."

But cookies wouldn't do much for strength. I found some power bars, and we ate those. Then I let Timmy have two cookies. I told him we had to save the rest — just in case.

Dad's head was all swollen under the bandage. His forehead had turned an awful purple around the cut. From the way his leg lay in the canoe, maybe that was broken too. He needed help, and fast. But the cell phone didn't work. And there was nobody in sight. Nobody at all.

"Okay, let's keep going," I said.

Timmy said nothing. I knew his arms were aching too. But we had no choice. We couldn't just sit out there and wait.

So we paddled. When we stopped for lunch, my hands were raw. I wrapped some bandages around them so I could keep on paddling.

"Are you real sure we're going the right way?" Timmy asked.

"Sure I'm sure," I lied. "We're just not going as fast as we came, that's all. The wind is against us and so is the current. We just have to keep on paddling."

"But we'll get back by dark, right?" Timmy asked.

"Yeah, for sure," I lied. "We'll find help before the sun sets."

CHAPTER 4

To Build a Fire

We didn't find help that day. We didn't make it back to the town of Pinehouse. We didn't seem to be getting anywhere.

The sun was setting when we gave up paddling. We pulled the canoe onto the shore and tied it up. Dad was still out cold. Timmy and I were beat.

"I thought you said . . ." Timmy began.

"Forget what I said," I shot back. "We're going against the current. We'll get back tomorrow, that's all."

My brother said nothing. I thought he might cry, but he didn't. Instead, he bit his bottom lip and tried to help. Our first job was to drag Dad out of the canoe. I thought my back would break, but we got him onto land. Then we unpacked our gear and found a dry spot for the sleeping bags. We had left the tent behind — a mistake!

Timmy went out to look for dry wood. I unwrapped my hands and stared at them. They were swollen and full of blisters. I'd never paddled for a whole day before. Now my hands were raw and my muscles ached.

Still, I was better off than my dad. I thought he might have a fever, but it was hard to tell. Half his head was a purple bruise. The other half was pale, almost white. He looked bad. Sometimes he'd wake up and moan. Most of the time he was out cold.

"Hang in there, Dad," I whispered. I knew he couldn't hear, but I went ahead. "We're going to make it. I promise you — we're going to make it."

Timmy came back with his arms full of wood. He made a pile and I found the matches. We had lots of waterproof matches. But we didn't have any dry paper to start the fire.

"We need kindling," I said.

"What's that?" Timmy asked.

"Little pieces of wood to start the fire. We'll both go look."

The best kindling is birch bark. We didn't find any. But we did get lots of small pine branches and dry pine needles. I found a knife and began cutting the pine into little bits. When the pile was ready, I tried to light it. A couple of pieces of bark flared up, but then the fire went out.

"Don't you have to blow on it?" Timmy asked.

"Yeah. I forgot," I said. *How come it was so easy when Dad did it?*

We tried again. This time I blew the fire right out. Then one more try, and slowly the fire grew. We kept feeding it bigger branches, then blowing on the flames. At last we had a real — but smoky — fire.

"Maybe someone will see the smoke," Timmy said.

"Yeah, maybe."

When I told Timmy to ditch half the food, he threw away the meat. That left us with bread, soup, peanut butter and jelly. It wasn't much of a dinner. We heated up the soup, then ate it from the can. Then we toasted peanut butter sandwiches. They were better with jelly on top. At the end, we ate most of the cookies.

By then, of course, we were beat. Timmy fell asleep with a cookie in his mouth. I put him in a sleeping bag. Then I looked around. *This could be beautiful*, I thought. *If Dad were okay. If we weren't lost. If we were just camping out.*

But I was tired, too. It was too late to tie our food up in the trees. Instead, I put the food in a pack and set it away from our camp.

The bugs came out when the sun set. They were coming at me like dive-bombers. I kept swatting at them when they landed on me. *Take that*, I said, killing one. *And you, too.* But there were a million

of them and just one of me.

I put a shirt over my dad and a blanket over Timmy. Then I climbed into my sleeping bag. I pulled a T-shirt over my face to keep off the bugs. Fat chance! The bugs kept biting right through the shirt.

I tried to sleep. I wished I could be like Timmy. He just conked out — dead to the world. But not me. I heard sounds in the night. There were *creaks* and *cricks* and scratching sounds.

Then I felt something on my ear. I reached up and there was a spider crawling on me. That made me sit right up — and the bugs were at me again.

Sleep? What is that? I asked myself. The night was full of noises. The ground was full of things that crawled. The air was full of things that bite. My mind was full of . . . everything.

But somehow I must have fallen asleep. In the early morning, I felt Timmy poking at me.

"Connor, wake up!" he whispered.

"Yeah, yeah," I replied. I blinked. The sun was just starting to rise over the lake.

"I hear something," Timmy went on.

"Yeah, yeah," I mumbled. But then I heard it too. The sound was like scratching. It was like a very big cat, scratching a couch. But there were no cats out here.

"Did you hang up the food?" Timmy asked.

I swore. That was answer enough.

We both rolled over and looked into the woods. There was nothing there — but then a shape, a dark shape.

"A bear?" Timmy asked.

I couldn't tell for sure, but what else could it be? I whispered to Timmy, "We've got to get out of here, like fast."

"How?"

"Leave everything," I said. "We lift Dad, put him in the canoe, then push off."

"Can bears swim?" Timmy asked.

"I don't want to find out."

CHAPTER 5

Another Day

We woke up fast, very fast. In a flash, we jumped from our sleeping bags. Then we picked up our Dad and rolled him into the canoe. Timmy jumped in the front. I pushed the back until the water was up to my waist. Then I pulled myself into the canoe.

When we were out in the water, my brother looked at the shore.

"Look, it's a baby," Timmy said.

I sat up in the back of the canoe. Back at our

camp, a bear cub was pawing our food. It was only as big as a large stuffed teddy bear.

"It's so cute," Timmy went on.

"It has a mother," I told him.

"And here she comes," Timmy laughed.

A bear cub really is cute. But a large female bear is not. The mother bear looked at the food, at her cub and at us. Maybe she was trying to make sense of it all. For a second, I thought she might come after us. Bears really can swim, I remembered. And they can climb trees. If a bear comes after you, it's bad news.

But mama bear didn't care about us. The jar of peanut butter must have looked and smelled better than we did. Baby bear was into our jam jar. We had given these guys a bear picnic.

"So much for our food," groaned Timmy.

"And all the rest. The map's back there. So are the sleeping bags."

"Yeah, but we'll reach town today," Timmy said. He looked at me, his eyes full of hope. I guess an eight-year-old believes what an older kid says.

"Yeah, right," I mumbled.

I tried to remember the map. We should be at the bottom end of the lake by now. Somehow we must have gone past the town. Or did we? And which way was north, anyhow?

Ah, moss grows on the north side of a tree! A sudden brain flash. So I looked for moss on trees, and there it was. But the shore kept going south. So we weren't at the bottom end of the lake yet.

"Which way?" Timmy asked.

"Follow the shore," I told him. I tried to sound sure of myself. But I had a sinking feeling in my gut.

It was hard paddling that day. The wind was against us. The current was against us. My hands felt like they were raw. And my dumb brother didn't help much. He kept seeing float planes up in the sky. He'd wave at them, as if they might really see us.

Now if Dad had brought a flare, I thought. But I said nothing. We paddled along the shore, looking off in the distance for the town or a camp or some smoke. Anything.

By noon, we were both starving. I had never been so hungry in all my life. We pulled the canoe over to the shore, then pulled it up on a rocky beach. Dad was still out cold. So we left him in the canoe.

It was easy to get water to drink. The water of Pinehouse Lake was clean. It tasted great. But food was something else.

"Come on," I told Timmy. "We'll pick some berries."

"Berries?" he whined.

"Yeah, berries or nothing. You can eat them or starve. Take your pick."

I guess I was angry at him. He hadn't paddled hard that morning. And Timmy kept goofing off. So I snapped at him, and that made him shut up.

We headed into the bush and found some berry bushes. We were in luck — the berries were ripe. They glowed red on the bushes.

"You sure these are good to eat?" Connor asked.

"Bears eat them," I said.

Timmy shrugged and began popping the berries into his mouth. I did the same. Pretty soon our hands and faces were stained red.

"You look like a vampire," I said.

"You, too," Connor replied. Then he licked the berry juice from his fingers.

We laughed. There was something so awful about all this that we just had to laugh.

After lunch — if you could call it lunch — we pushed off from the shore. Some clouds had come up and it began to rain. *Great*, I said to myself. *All this, and now we're getting soaked.*

I really did think we'd get somewhere that day. We paddled until our hands were like raw meat. My shoulders ached. Even my butt and knees hurt. But we saw nothing on the shore, nothing ahead of us. The rain kept falling, and our hopes seemed to get washed away.

I think it was five o'clock when I heard Timmy sniffling. He was up at the front of the canoe, so I couldn't see him.

"Timmy, are you okay?" I asked him.

"Yes . . ." he said at first. Then he turned back to me and I saw the hurt in his eyes. He'd been crying, but in the rain I couldn't see his tears. "No . . ." he said, and then he began wailing.

"Crying won't do any good," I said.

"But what . . . what are we going to do?" he wailed. "We've got no food. We're lost. Dad's sick . . ." and then the tears began again.

"It'll be okay," I told him.

"Connor, I'm scared," my brother cried.

I said nothing more. The simple truth was too awful to say out loud. I was scared too.

CHAPTER 6

Give Me Shelter

That night was the worst night of our lives. The rain kept falling. We had matches, but we couldn't get a fire going. We had no food.

And we were sick.

It must have been the berries. I threw up first, then Timmy. By dinner time, we were puking our guts out.

So we didn't really want to eat. Maybe that was the good news. Instead, we listened to the rain fall. We shook in the cold. And we threw up.

"You said the berries were good to eat," Timmy whined.

"Yeah, I thought they were," I snapped back. "And I ate them too, you know."

"Are we going to get back?" he asked.

"Yeah. Tomorrow," I said. I tried to sound sure of myself.

"And Dad?"

"He'll be fine," I said. I wasn't sure about that, but that's what I told Timmy. "Right now, he's better than we are."

Dad was better — he really was. He could open his eyes and at least groan. That was better than being out cold. Still, we couldn't ask him for help. I don't think he knew where we were or what had happened.

After sunset, the bugs came out again. We had no tent. We had nothing but our wet clothes and our canoe. I made a shelter by turning the canoe over. Then we made a kind of bed out of pine branches. When all that was done, I pulled my shirt over my head and tried to sleep.

How can a guy sleep when a million bugs are dive-bombing him? I tossed and turned all night. I wondered if it would be better to give up. I wondered if we'd ever get home. You get some really bad thoughts at night.

I woke up in the morning when I heard a sound. It was like a large animal stepping on a tree branch. *A bear,* I thought.

I sat up, shaking.

In front of me was Timmy, smiling.

"You look scared," he said.

"I had a dream," I told him, "about a bear. I thought . . . oh, never mind."

"Anyhow, Dad's awake," Timmy said brightly.

My dad really was awake, all right. His eyes were open and glassy. He seemed to be shaking from cold.

"Dad, are you okay?" I asked him.

He opened his mouth, but the words must have hurt him. "N-no," he groaned. "N-need help."

"We're going to get help," I told him. "Today."

That's what I said, but I wasn't really sure. We should have got to Pinehouse the day before. We could have paddled all the way back to our car by now. But we were nowhere. In fact, I had no idea where we were.

We gave Dad some water to drink, then got ready to head off. There was no sense eating, and we both felt pretty sick. *Better just go,* I told myself. *Go somewhere.*

We kept rowing along the shore. It seemed a

little easier today. There was no wind, and the rain had stopped. It even felt like the current was behind us. That didn't make sense to me, of course. If I was right, we should still be paddling against the current. But we had no map and no compass, so how could I tell?

"Look, bears!" Timmy called out around noon.

"Yeah, look at that," I said. I put down my oar and rested. "It looks like the bear family that came into our camp."

"Could they be following us?" he asked.

"Nah, bears aren't that smart," I told him. But I wasn't really sure about that.

"And look over there," Timmy said. "A jar of peanut butter. And some ripped up sleeping bags. It looks like. . ."

He didn't say it. I didn't say it. But the truth hit us both at the same time. *We were back at our camp.* We had paddled for a day and a half, and ended up where we started.

That's when I lost it. All that paddling, all that work, and we had gone nowhere. We were tired,

cold and starving — and we'd gone nowhere.

I started to cry. I tried to fight it, but the whole thing was just too awful. I cried and then I sobbed like a baby. I felt like a fool — and idiot.

"Connor, it'll be okay," Timmy said. This time he was the strong one and I was the guy who cried.

"No, it won't," I moaned. "We're lost. We've got nothing. We don't know what to do."

"Hey, stop crying," Timmy said. "We're going to

be okay. Dad's awake now. He'll help us get back."

I looked at my dad in the center of the canoe. He was on his back, facing up at the sky. His eyes were pale, the color of the sky. His mouth was half open and he was still shaking from cold.

"Dad," I croaked, "we're lost. What should we do?"

For a little while, I thought our Dad might say something. But no, he closed his eyes and went back to sleep.

That's when Timmy had a brainwave. "I've got an idea," he said. "The planes that fly over us — they're all flying out of La Ronge. I mean, they're flying into La Ronge, or taking off. . ."

"I get it," I said. "The planes are flying out northwest, so we just have to follow them."

"It's easy," Timmy said.

And it was easy, but it had taken us two days to think of it.

The planes flew lower as they got near the airport, higher when they flew off. So we set our course by watching the first plane that flew over.

49

The new course, however, wasn't along the shore. It was across the middle of the lake. We put on our life jackets, but still it was scary. Soon we were a long way from shore and moving fast.

"We're going to make it," Timmy said.

And maybe we were. We didn't have to paddle very hard. The current was with us, even in the lake. The canoe kept moving, going . . . somewhere. It felt like we were making progress.

In a couple of hours, we came to the other side of the lake. Up ahead of us was where the lake emptied into a river. The current was moving fast now.

And then it hit me.

"I know where we are," I told Timmy. "We've been here before, remember?"

Timmy gave me a blank look. He didn't remember. It was four years ago, on a different trip.

"It's the Trapper River," I told him. "It leads to the Churchill River up north."

"I remember now," Timmy said. "We didn't canoe here. We went over the land."

"You remember why?"

"The rapids," Timmy whispered. His voice was full of fear. "The Bus Cruncher Rapids are just ahead!"

CHAPTER 7

The Bus Cruncher Rapids

The Trapper River goes from Pinehouse Lake up north. It feeds into another lake, and then into the Churchill River. We'd been on the Trapper River before, a few years ago. We canoed the easy part. The water was fast, but smooth. With the current behind us, it was easy.

But we did a portage around the Bus Cruncher Rapids. The name is enough to tell why. Dad said that the water was so fast and wild it would crunch a bus. So we did a portage with our canoe. A

portage is when you carry the canoe over the land.
It's a lot of work, but sometimes you have to do it.
When the river is too shallow, or too rocky, or too
fast — well, there's no choice.

I remembered that portage. Timmy, of course,
wanted to shoot the rapids. He had this thing
about whitewater. My dad just told us we'd get
killed. So Dad carried the canoe to smooth water. I
helped him. Timmy whined.

"Okay, let's get to the shore," I shouted. "No way we're shooting the Bus Cruncher."

"I'm trying," Timmy shouted back.

"Try harder," I yelled.

The current gets faster when you come close to rapids. It can really push a canoe. Up ahead, I could see the spray of water hitting rocks. That's what whitewater is. The water hits the rocks and turns white or sprays up in the air.

You can take a canoe through some whitewater. My dad had done some of that but never with us. He said we were too young. He said our canoe might break in half. I looked up at the whitewater ahead. No, we weren't going to tackle that.

"Aim for the shore," I yelled again.

"You steer the back!" Timmy yelled back.

He was right. In fast water, you steer from the back, not the front. So I dug into the water with my paddle. Our back end swung to the right, but it swung too far. We hit a swirl in the water. And then we were going sideways!

"Switch your paddle," I screamed. "Paddle right!"

Timmy did. We both paddled like crazy. In a minute, we had the canoe under control, but that minute cost us. We were at the start of the rapids.

"It's too late. We can't get to shore!" Timmy yelled.

That was the truth. We were in the middle of the river, with rock ledges on both sides. Up ahead, the water swirled over rocks. Spray and foam shot up when the water hit a rock. And we were moving fast.

"Okay, we can do this," I shouted to Timmy. I wasn't sure he could hear me. The river sounded like thunder as it hit the rocks. "You tell me what's coming. I'll steer."

That's how to handle fast water. But what else? I tried to remember what to do. *Look at the blue water, not the rocks.* Some old guy told me that. A canoe will go where your eyes go. If you look at the rocks, you'll hit the rocks. If you look at the way through, you'll make it.

"Just tell me where the blue water is," I shouted. "That's all I need to know."

We were moving like crazy. I had never gone so fast in a canoe before. The water pushed us like a speedboat. Around us, the water crashed into rocks at the shore. Spray shot up and fell down on us.

I thought, *this is like a fun park*. But this was not a fun park ride, this was real. Boats crash in whitewater. People get thrown by whitewater. People die in whitewater. We had a chance — but only a chance — of coming out alive.

Rocks are what make the water spray up. In rapids like these, the rocks are all over. They poke up from the river bottom. Some are like fists, some like knives. Some will turn a canoe over. Some will cut right through it.

"Go right," Timmy screamed.

So I paddled like crazy. I tried to get power from each stroke. Push, down, over, again. We had to stay in the blue water, but it was hard. So hard.

"Left," he yelled. "Hard left!"

I dug in the paddle and we went left. Then I heard the sound: *scrunch*. The canoe had scraped against a big rock.

"Right, right!" Timmy yelled.

Again I dug in the paddle. I pulled the boat right, somehow.

"Good, now easy left."

We were okay so far. The water was fast but not awful. We scraped over a few rocks but none that tipped us too far.

"More left. Fast!" Timmy screamed.

I did a reverse paddle. That really turns the boat. But I didn't want to get us sideways again.

"Almost there!"

Almost, but not quite. We got too close to a big rock. It scraped right along the side of the canoe. But we didn't turn over. We were doing okay. Up ahead, I could see the end of the rapids. The blue water could get us there. We just had to stay on course.

That's when Timmy stopped paddling. He turned towards me. "We made it!" he cried.

"Keep paddling," I shouted. But it was too late.

The front of the canoe turned right. I tried to fix that from the back, but I couldn't. Up ahead I saw a large rock, the last of the big ones. If I could just move the canoe in time, we'd be okay.

I saw the rock. I saw the blue water, but I kept looking at the rock. If I could just . . .

BAM!

CHAPTER 8

Into the Water

The water came like a fist into my mouth and nose. I was under the water, bubbles all around me. I kept twisting and turning. I was being pushed by the current, helpless. Then I scraped the bottom and pushed up.

Air! I can breathe!

I took a breath, but water came with it. I was under again, dragged against my will.

Swim, I told myself. But the current was too

strong to swim. I kept my hands out in front of me.
So long as I don't hit a rock, I said to myself.

And then I hit a rock — head first. I was gone.

*   *   *

Some campers had seen us coming. They were at the end of the rapids, by the calm water. They saw our canoe coming down the rapids. And they thought we were crazy.

But when our canoe turned over, it was the campers who saved us. They came into the water and grabbed me and Timmy. Then they pulled my dad from the water. In a few minutes, we were all on shore. We were wet, and hurt, but alive.

The campers had a satellite phone. They called for help and a float plane came in pretty quickly. By then, my brother, my father and I were all wrapped in blankets. We were getting warm by a fire. Even my dad must have been better. He told us another bad joke.

Back in La Ronge, Dad had to stay three days in hospital. He really conked his head with that fall. He also broke a couple of ribs. We don't know if that was from the fall or from turning over in the rapids.

Timmy and I were mostly okay. I had smashed my face into a rock, but that was all. Timmy was still sick from the berries, but he got over that. In a few days, we were in pretty good shape.

Of course, our mom was mad. I mean, first she was happy that we were all alive. But then she got mad, the way moms do. She told my father that he could have killed us. She blamed him for not being careful. She said that there'd be no more canoe trips unless she came along.

Great, I groaned.

"But we did shoot the Bus Cruncher Rapids, Mom," Timmy told her.

"Almost," she replied.

"Okay, almost. If we took that whitewater course, we could have done it."

My mom just looked at him. She knew what was coming.

Timmy gave her this big grin. "So next summer, maybe instead of a canoe trip . . . "

"We take a course," I finished for him. "A whitewater course."

My mom sighed. I wasn't sure if that was a yes or a no. But Dad said he'd talk to her. Maybe, just maybe . . .

The Crash

by PAUL KROPP

A school bus slides off a cliff in a snowstorm. The bus driver is out cold. One of the guys is badly hurt. Can Craig, Rory and Lerch find help in time?

Three Feet Under

by PAUL KROPP

Scott and Rico find a map to long-lost treasure. There's $250,000 buried in Bolton's mine. But when the school bully steals their map and heads for the old mine, the race is on.

Bats Past Midnight

by SHARON JENNINGS

Sam and Simon wonder about a fancy car that hangs around their school late at night. When they try to find out more, they end up in trouble at school, at home and with the police.

Bats in the Graveyard

by SHARON JENNINGS

Sam and Simon (the "Bat gang") have to look after Sam's younger sister on Halloween night. Soon they all end up in the graveyard — spooked!

Pump

by SHARON JENNING

Just enter the half-pipe in a crouch. Then rise to a standing position as you begin the upward slope. A pump is easy, not like the rest of Pat's life.

Our Plane Is Down

by DOUG PATON

A small plane goes down in the bush, hours from anywhere. The radio is broken, the pilot is out cold. There's only a little water and even less food. Can Cal make it through the woods to save his sister, the pilot and himself?

Avalanche

by PAUL KROPP

It was just a school trip, just a winter hike through the mountains. But when a wall of snow comes sliding down, fifteen kids have to fight for their lives. Not all of them will win the fight.

Against All Odds

by PAUL KROPP

Nothing ever came easy for Jeff. He had a tough time at school and hung around with all the wrong kids in the neighborhood. But when he and his brother are drowning in a storm sewer, Jeff is the one who never gives up.

Paul Kropp is the author of more than fifty novels for young people. His work includes nine award-winning young adult novels, many high-interest novels, as well as books and stories for both adults and early readers.

Paul Kropp's best-known novels for young adults, *Moonkid and Liberty* and *Moonkid and Prometheus*, have been translated into many languages and have won awards around the world. His high-interest novels have sold nearly a million copies in Canada and the United States. For more information on Paul, visit his website at www.paulkropp.com.